Not Me!

Nigel McMullen

Dutton Children's Books
New York

Jack says Kenny is the best brother in the world. At breakfast, when Jack knocked his plate on the floor and Mom came in, looking angry...

Jack said, "It was him!"

Kenny, who was too young
to talk, said nothing.

At lunchtime, when Mom asked who had eaten the cake she'd taken all morning to bake...

Jack said, "Not me!" and hid
the last slice in Kenny's diaper.

Kenny, who was too young to care, sat down.

Jack was making mud pies
when Mom called,
"You'd better stay clean!"

Jack said, "I will," and
wiped his hands on Kenny's shirt.

Kenny, who was
too young to know
what mud was,
thought it
tasted lovely.

At bath time, Jack
was playing with
the squirty soap when
Mom asked who'd made
all the mess....

Jack said, "It was him!" and handed the bottle to Kenny.

Splosh!

Kenny, who was too young to know better, squirted Mom.

When they were warm and sleepy and ready for bed, Mom looked at Kenny and sighed, "You're so much trouble! But we wouldn't trade him, would we, Jack?"

Jack said, "Not me!" and gave Kenny a kiss.

Kenny, who had never said
anything before, chose that
moment to say his very first word...